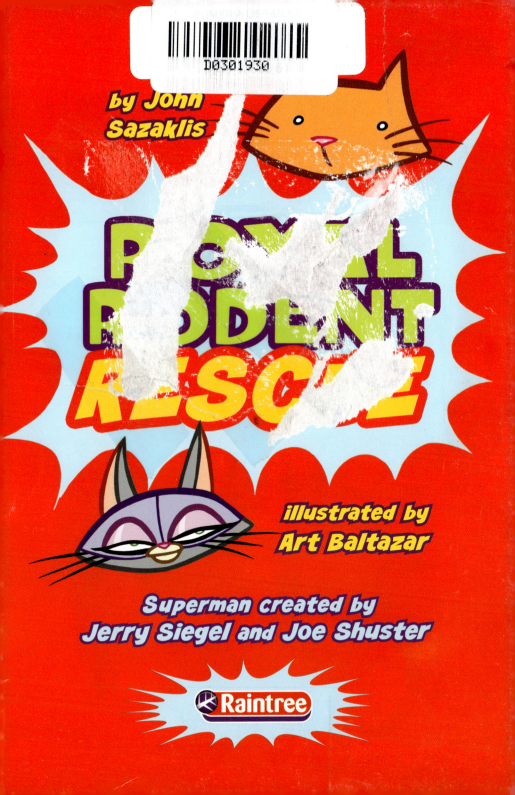

by John Sazaklis

ROYAL RODENT RESCUE

illustrated by
Art Baltazar

Superman created by
Jerry Siegel and Joe Shuster

Raintree

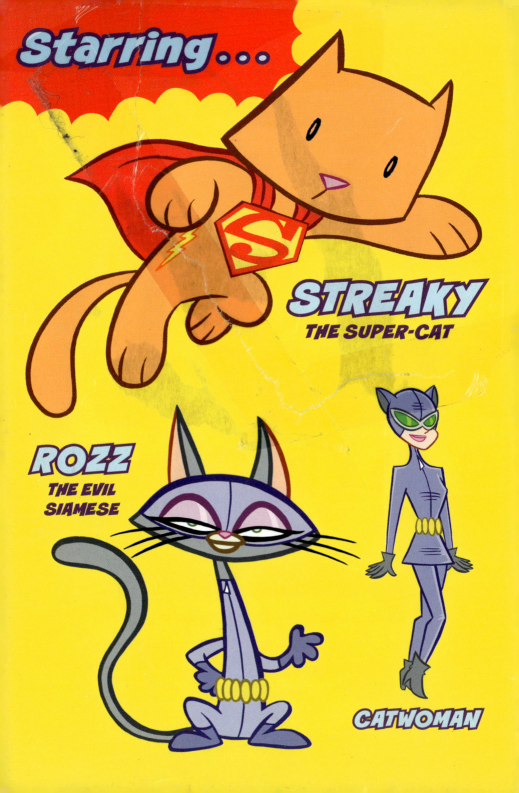

CONTENTS

FORTRESS of SOLITUDE SUPER-COMPUTER

SUPER-PET HERO FILE 004:

STREAKY

heat vision

X-ray vision

super-hearing

super-strong tail

super-breath

S-shield

lightning bolt

flight

Super hero owner:
SUPERGIRL

Species: Super-Cat

Place of birth: Earth

Age: unknown

Favourite foods: milk and sushi

Bio: While performing an experiment, Supergirl turned her pet cat into a Super-Cat! Streaky has the same powers as the Girl of Steel.

CAT OF STEEL

High above the city of Metropolis, **Streaky the Super-Cat** zoomed through the air. His super-hearing had picked up the siren of a fire truck.

He followed the sound to a burning building.

When the Cat of Steel arrived, he saw a fireman on the roof.

"The building is empty!" the fireman cried. Then he ran over to a ladder resting against the wall.

Suddenly, the fire reached a gas pipe. **KA-BOOM!**

The blast sent the fireman flying. He landed in a nearby tree.

Streaky flew into the building. He used his super-breath to put out the flames. **FWOOOM!**

Then with his teeth, Streaky

picked up the fireman by his coat.

The Super-Cat carried him to safety.

"Would you look at that?" said the

fire chief. **"That's the first time a**

cat has got one of us out of a tree!"

"HOORAY!"

The nearby crowd began to cheer.

The firemen took turns petting Streaky.

They scratched him under his chin.

The feline hero purred with satisfaction

at another job well done.

Then Streaky flicked his tail. He

flew up, up, and away. **ZOOM!**

Soon his cape was just a red spot in

the blue sky.

Reaching the **Fortress of Solitude,**

Streaky let out a deep breath.

"All that hero work is tiring," Streaky said. "And you know what that means? **It's time for a nap!**"

Streaky curled up in a special part of the Fortress. His

owner, Supergirl, had made the spot just for him. After cleaning his fur, Streaky closed his eyes and fell asleep.

An alarm rang through the Fortress of Solitude.

Streaky leapt out of bed and into the

air. He held on to the icy ceiling with

his claws.

"What's going on?" Streaky cried.

The Super-Cat flew over to a computer in the main room of the Fortress. He rubbed his eyes. On the screen was a live shot of Metropolis. The giant robot villain Metallo was smashing his way through the city.

Streaky fixed his red cape. He headed to the exit. Then the image on the computer changed. Supergirl appeared. The Girl of Steel was fighting the robot.

"That's more like it!" Streaky said. The cat went back to bed.

In Gotham City, **Rozz the Siamese cat** paced around a hideout. Her owner, the evil **Catwoman**, admired stolen jewellery in a mirror.

On most days, Rozz would help
Catwoman with crimes. But today,
Batgirl was searching for them. They
had to stay hidden. Rozz was getting
really bored.

Catwoman turned on the TV to see
if her robbery had made the news.
Instead, she saw the video of Supergirl
fighting Metallo in Metropolis.

BANG! SMASH! CRASH!

Suddenly, a great shadow filled
the screen. It was the shadow of the
Batplane!

Batgirl had come to help her super-hero friend. Together, the World's Finest Heroes stopped the robot monster!

"With Batgirl in Metropolis, Gotham City is mine for the taking," Catwoman said. She jumped on to the window ledge. "When the Bat's away, this Cat will play!"

The villain leapt from the window. She fled into the night.

Rozz was excited by what she saw
on TV. A whole new city was out there
to explore. She packed a bag and put
it over her shoulder. Then she left the
hideout and headed to the bus stop.

Rozz was going to Metropolis!

CAT BURGLAR

Soon the bus reached the city. Rozz hopped off. She had been hiding in the luggage rack.

As she stretched her legs, Rozz took in the sights. Unlike Gotham City, Metropolis was shiny and clean. It looked brand new. **PURRR!**

The setting sun glowed on the tall buildings. The shops were closing. People were going home. The city became calm and quiet.

This place is pretty boring without crime, Rozz thought.

The Siamese cat decided to make her own fun. Rozz hopped on to the fence of a nearby building. She began to sing. She thought she had a lovely singing voice. The man who stuck his head out of a nearby window did not think so.

 he shouted.

"Tough crowd," Rozz said to herself.

She sang louder.

"Scat, cat!" the man

yelled. He threw a shoe at Rozz.

The shoe whizzed past her head. It

smashed through the window of an

electronics shop. The alarm sounded.

The man gasped. He shut his window

and turned off the lights.

"That's my signal to leave!" Rozz said. She ran down an alley.

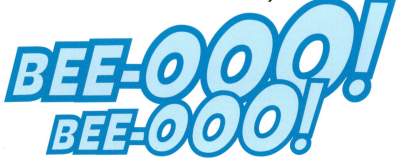

Another alarm sounded in the Fortress of Solitude. Streaky got up and rubbed his eyes. A break-in at an electronics shop. He knew it was his turn to save the day.

When Streaky got to the shop, the owner was holding a shoe. He was talking to Police Constable Merkel.

"Nothing was stolen, officer," said the shop owner. "But my window is broken."

"We'll find the criminal," replied PC Merkel. "No need to worry."

Streaky saw that everything was under control. He curled up on top of a TV. The Super-Cat continued his nap. If he was needed, he would be close by to help.

Meanwhile, Rozz searched for a place to spend the night. She came upon the Harper Hotel. The hotel had marble steps and a fancy fountain.

"This will do!" Rozz said to herself.

In front of the hotel, a limo pulled up. Rozz hid behind a step and watched. Several photographers ran out of the hotel. Camera flashes lit up the sky as the passengers stepped out of the car. Dressed in red robes, King Sandy and Queen Markela of Kardamyla greeted the crowd.

As the royal family entered the hotel, Rozz saw the queen carrying a cushion. A ball of brown fur sat on top. It was the queen's hamster, Prince Zouli. He was sound asleep.

Rozz's eyes widened.

MEOWW!

"That royal rodent will fetch me a king's ransom!" Rozz said.

Everyone knew Queen Markela's riches came from the trees found on her island. Their sweet sap was used to make many products, such as soap, lotion, and toothpaste. It was also used to make chewing gum, bread, and sweet treats.

Rozz had only dreamed of such gifts. Her stomach rumbled at the thought.

Rozz hurried into the hotel. A group of waiters and porters followed the royal family. They were carrying luggage and pushing trolleys of food.

Rozz hopped on a passing trolley. She enjoyed the ride. **She would soon have her paws on Prince Zouli!**

A few hours later, the king and queen were asleep. Prince Zouli the hamster did not sleep at night. Instead, he went looking for a food trolley. The prince climbed up the trolley to a plate of cheese.

Suddenly, he was snatched by a powerful set of claws! Rozz dropped Zouli into her bag. She climbed down the fire escape.

The hotel would soon be filled with police.

Once Rozz was on the street, something caught her eye. Next to the hotel was the perfect place to hide – **Papa Duke's Pet Shop!** Rozz found her way in. She locked up the prince in an empty birdcage. She smiled.

"You'll never get away with this!" squeaked Prince Zouli. "The pets of my country will come to Metropolis! They'll make you pay!"

"Relax, rat," hissed Rozz. She flashed her claws at the poor little hamster. *"Or else!"*

RODENT RESCUE

The next day, Streaky was startled awake once again. He looked up from his napping place in the electronics shop. A crowd of worried customers stood around a wall of television sets. Each TV was tuned to the WKAT News channel.

On each screen, an image of King Sandy and Queen Markela appeared. They looked upset. Their pet hamster, Prince Zouli, had been taken in the night.

Suddenly, a Siamese cat hopped on to the news desk. The cat looked over at the cameras. She meowed and waved her paws wildly.

"Meoww! Meowww!"

Humans could not understand the evil feline. But Streaky heard the message loud and clear.

"**Pets of Metropolis,**" said the cat on screen. **"My name is Rozz. These are my demands!"**

Rozz asked for a large number of gifts. She wanted a lifetime supply of treats from the royal family's island.

Rozz was planning to steal from Zouli's kingdom! Streaky had to find the hamster prince. He had to stop this crazy cat.

Using his super-hearing, the Cat of Steel picked up the signal from the TV station. Streaky zoomed into the sky. He followed it.

The Super-Cat blasted into the news station. As the dust cleared, Streaky landed proudly on the news desk.

"Show's over, Rozz!" shouted Streaky.

"You must belong to Supergirl," said Rozz. "The hero of Metropolis."

"That's right," said Streaky. "Now tell me where the prince is located. We'll settle this quietly."

"I don't think so," purred the Siamese. **"The fun has just begun!"**

Rozz reached into her bag. She pulled out a collar. Dangling from it was a glowing piece of green rock.

Kryptonite!

Rozz held the collar out to Streaky.

The green rock made the Super-Cat's

powers weak.

"I work for Catwoman. She has evil

friends," said Rozz. "That's how I got

my paws on this rock."

"I suggest you keep your distance, Super-Cat," Rozz laughed. **"You're looking a little green."**

Rozz hopped off the desk. Streaky was too weak to chase her. The Siamese cat burglar leapt through the hole in the wall. She was gone.

Moments later, Streaky's strength returned. He flew out of the TV station. Rozz was nowhere to be found. The Cat of Steel used his super-smelling to pick up the villain's scent. He followed the trail to Papa Duke's Pet Shop.

Streaky climbed into an air vent. Using his X-ray vision, he looked through the metal vent and into the store. Across the room, Prince Zouli was locked in a birdcage. Directly underneath, Rozz sat on top of a large fish tank. She was looking for a snack.

The Super-Cat acted fast. He aimed his heat vision at the cage. He blasted two energy beams at the lock.

The cage door flew open. Then the royal rodent made a run for it.

"Drat that rat!" Rozz yelled. She chased after Zouli. Then she grabbed the hamster. Rozz showed her claws.

The prince was in danger! Streaky needed to get close, but Rozz still held the kryptonite collar. The Super-Cat scanned the room. He had an idea.

WOOOOOSH!

Streaky zoomed over to a stack of kitty litter bags. He landed on them with all his weight. A cloud of dust filled the shop.

Rozz dropped Zouli. She turned to Streaky and hissed.

"You like to make an entrance, don't you, Super-Cat?" Rozz said. **"Well, now it's time to make your exit!"** The evil feline leapt on to the Cat of Steel.

The kryptonite collar was too much for Streaky. He started to black out.

Prince Zouli knew the collar was hurting Streaky. He raced up to Rozz. He grabbed the collar with his little paws. Using his sharp teeth, Zouli bit through the strap.

MUNCH! MUNCH! MUNCH!

The collar fell out of Rozz's grasp. The hamster ran with it to the exit. He squeezed under the door and into the street. Once outside, Zouli dropped the collar down a drain.

Streaky's powers returned. In a flash, Rozz found herself inside the empty birdcage. Streaky bent the bars shut around her. She was trapped.

"Looks like your criminal career is for the birds," Streaky said to Rozz.

Streaky turned to Prince Zouli. "Thanks for your help, your majesty," he said to the hamster prince.

"I was only returning the favour, dear friend," Prince Zouli replied.

Streaky put Prince Zouli on his back. He flew the royal hamster back to the hotel. The king and queen were overjoyed at the return of their pet. They showered Streaky with gifts.

Streaky curled up on the king's pillow. **A nap was the best gift of all.**

*   *   *

The next morning, Papa Duke opened his pet shop. He was surprised to find a mess of kitty litter on the floor. He was more surprised to find a Siamese cat trapped in a birdcage.

Rozz clawed at the man as he lifted her out. Then he placed her in a cage filled with baby kittens. The cute critters quickly warmed up to the angry Siamese. They pulled on her ears. They climbed on her back. Rozz could hardly stand it.

"**Well, you wanted excitement,**"

Rozz said to herself. "**Try getting**

yourself out of this one."

THE END

KNOW YOUR

Krypto

Streaky

Beppo

Comet

Ace

Jumpa

Whatzit

B'dg

Storm

Topo

Ark

Hoppy

Paw Pooch

Bull Dog

Chameleon Collie

Hot Dog

These are **HERO** PETS.

Tail Terrier

Tusky Husky

SUPER-PETS

Ignatius

Chauncey

Crackers

Giggles

Artie Puffin

Griff

Waddles

Rozz

Dex-Starr

Glomulus

Misty

Sneezers

Whoosh

Pronto

Snorrt

Rolf

Squealer

Kajunn

These are **VILLAIN** PETS.

GLOSSARY

burglar someone who steals things

electronics devices powered by electricity, such as computers, TVs, and radios

Fortress of Solitude secret headquarters of Supergirl

porter employee who is in charge of the entrance of a hotel

ransom money that is demanded before someone being held can be set free

Siamese cat slender breed of cat with short hair and a pale brown or grey coat. A Siamese cat's ears, paws, and tail are often dark.

villain evil person or animal

MEET THE AUTHOR

John Sazaklis

John Sazaklis spent some of his life working in a coffee shop called the House of Doughnuts. The rest of it, he spent drawing and writing stories. He has illustrated Spider-Man books and written Batman books. He has also created toys used in *MAD Magazine.*

MEET THE ILLUSTRATOR

Eisner Award-winner Art Baltazar

Art Baltazar defines cartoons and comics not only as a style of art, but as a way of life. Art is the creative force behind *The New York Times* best-selling, Eisner Award-winning, DC Comics series Tiny Titans and the co-writer for *Billy Batson and the Magic of SHAZAM!* Art draws comics and never has to leave the house. He lives with his lovely wife, Rose, big boy Sonny, little boy Gordon, and little girl Audrey.

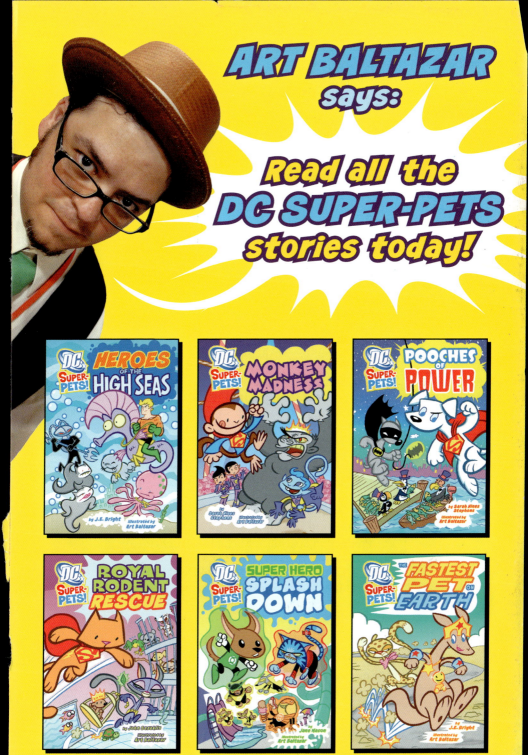

www.raintreepublishers.co.uk
Visit our website to find out
more information about
Raintree books.

To order:
☎ Phone 0845 6044371
🖷 Fax +44 (0) 1865 312263
🖳 Email myorders@raintreepublishers.co.uk

Customers from outside the UK please telephone +44 1865 312262

Raintree is an imprint of Capstone Global Library Limited,
a company incorporated in England and Wales having its registered office at
7 Pilgrim Street, London, EC4V 6LB – Registered company number: 6695582

First published by Picture Window Books in 2011
First published in the United Kingdom in 2012
The moral rights of the proprietor have been asserted.

STAR26255

Art Director and Designer: Bob Lentz
Editors: Donald Lemke and Vaarunika Dharmapala
Production Specialist: Michelle Biedscheid
Creative Director: Heather Kindseth
Editorial Director: Michael Dahl
Printed and bound in China by Leo Paper Products Ltd

ISBN 978 1 406 23649 1 (paperback)
15 14 13 12 11
10 9 8 7 6 5 4 3 2 1

British Library Cataloguing in Publication Data
A full catalogue record for this book is available from the British Library.